ght Fire

Written and Illustrated
by Lori Lukasewich

Stoddart
Kids

TORONTO • NEW YORK

Published in Canada in 2001 by
Stoddart Kids,
a division of Stoddart Publishing Co. Limited
895 Don Mills Road, 400-2 Park Centre
Toronto, Ontario M3C 1W3
Tel (416) 445-3333 Fax (416) 445-5967
E-mail cservice@ genpub.com

Distributed in Canada by
General Distribution Services
325 Humber College Blvd.,
Toronto, ON M9W 7C3
Tel (416) 213-1919 Fax (416) 213-1917
E-mail cservice@ genpub.com

Published in the United States in 2001 by
Stoddart Kids,
a division of Stoddart Publishing Co. Limited
180 Varick Street, 9th Floor
New York, New York 10014
Toll free 1-800-805-1083
E-mail gdsinc@genpub.com

Distributed in the United States by
General Distribution Services
4500 Witmer Industrial Estates, PMB 128
Niagara Falls, New York 14305-1386
Toll free 1-800-805-1083
E-mail gdsinc@genpub.com

Canadian Cataloguing in Publication Data

Lukasewich, Lori, 1953–
The night fire

ISBN 0-7737-3296-9

I. Title.

PS8573.U5353N53 2001   jC811'.6   C00-932986-2
PZ8.3.L84Ni 2001

A visit to a fire hall on a busy night in the lives of the firefighters.

Printed and bound in Hong Kong, China

THE CANADA COUNCIL | LE CONSEIL DES ARTS
FOR THE ARTS | DU CANADA
SINCE 1957 | DEPUIS 1957

*We acknowledge for their financial support of our
publishing program the Canada Council, the Ontario Arts
Council, and the Government of Canada through the
Book Publishing Industry Development Program (BPIDP).*

Acknowledgements

I would like to thank the following important people without
whose help and encouragement I couldn't have finished this
book: my dear husband, Lawrence, for the time, love, and
constant support, our boys, Carl, Micah, and Noel, for time
(cooking and cleaning), Emily and Levi Halvorson for fridge
drawings and magnets, my agent, Johanna Bates, for believ-
ing in me, Brad Harris for his amazing facility with words
and his perseverance on my behalf. And my dad, Bill Ellis,
for really annoying comments and laughter.

To the memory of my mother, Anna Margreta Ellis, who,
through varying degrees of understanding what I was doing
or why I was doing it,
never wavered or stinted in her ongoing love and support.
I love you, Mom, wherever you are.
Thanks, with all my heart.

Above the fire hall nighttime comes
and wraps itself around the sun.

While safe inside, the engines gleam
As firefighters wash them clean.

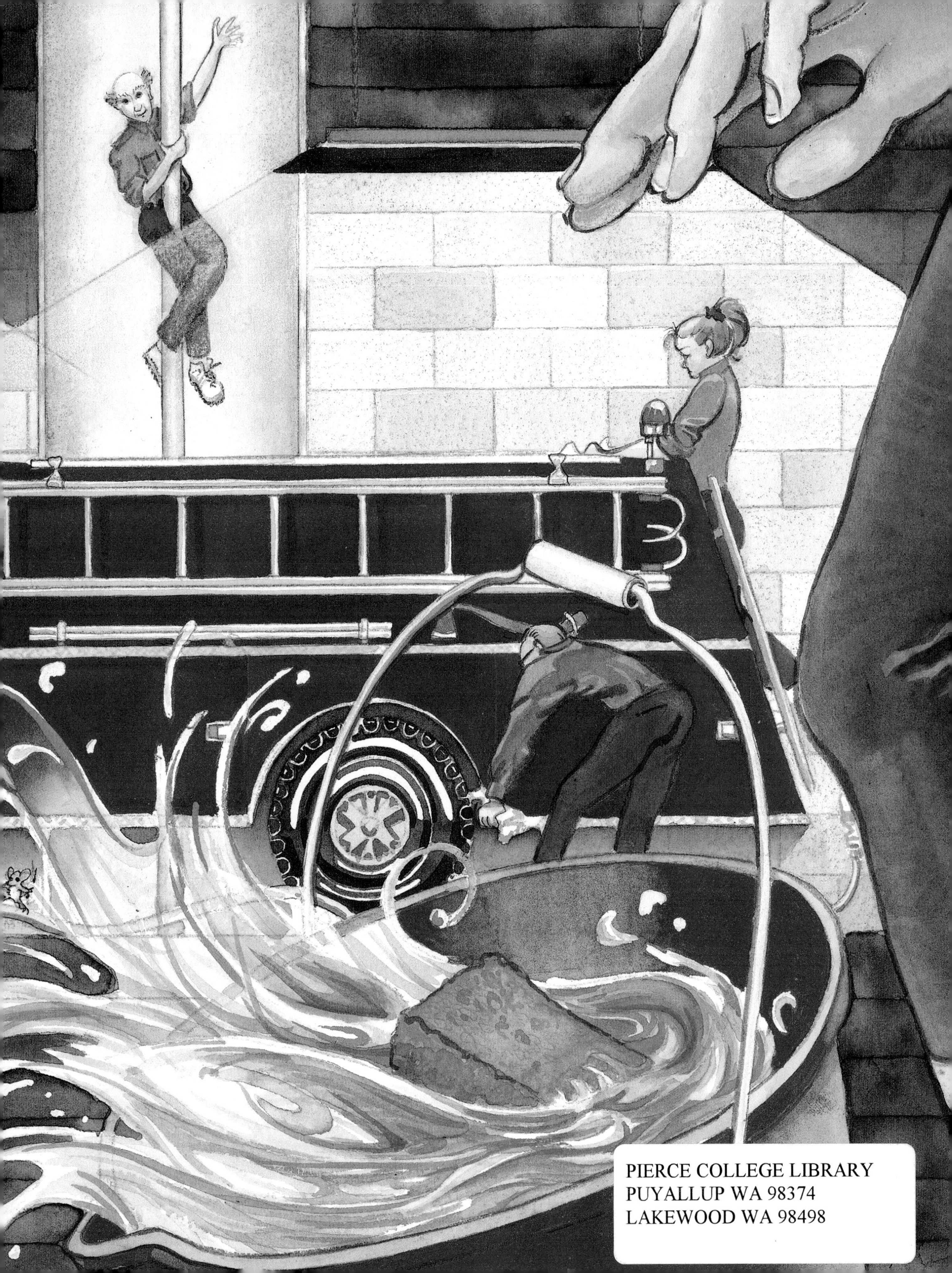

And when they finish up the job,
They play Go Fish . . . read . . . feed the dog.

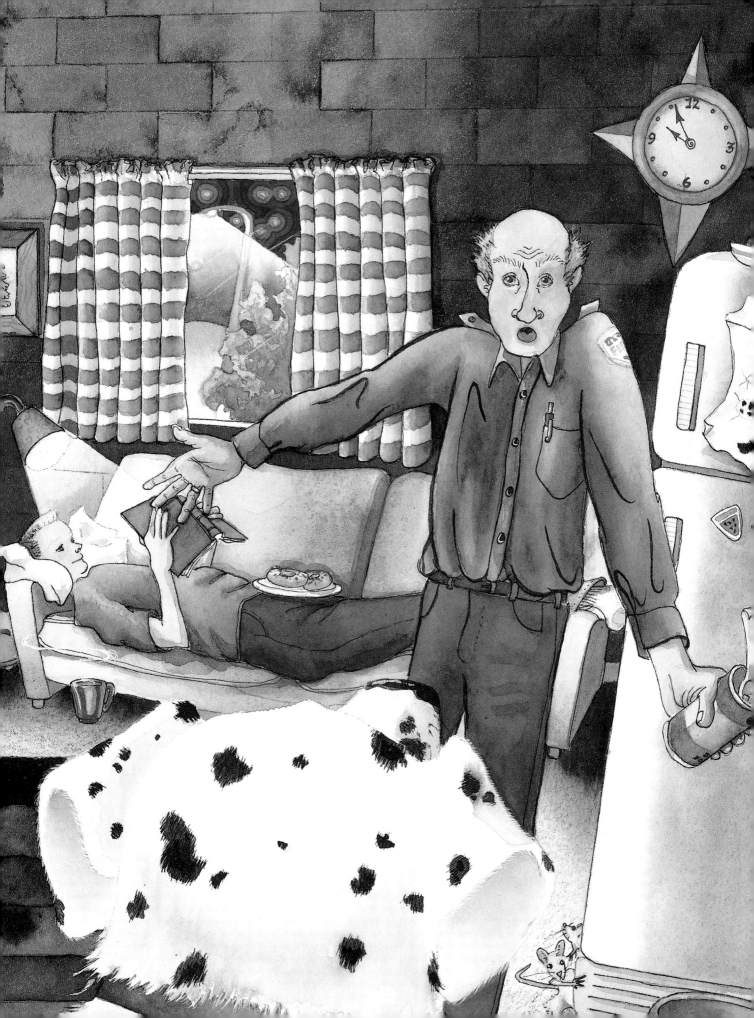

Then all at once alarm bells sound.
"Our house is burning to the ground!"

"Tell us where, we have to know!"
They check the map and quickly go!

The tires squeal, the sirens blare.
The driver shouts, "I see it! There!"

"Save the people! Get them out!
Are you all right?" their neighbors shout.

With tears and cheers and worried faces
The neighbors give them warm embraces.

The fire is hot, the smoke is thick.
Firefighters work in spite of it.

They put it out and pack their gear,
"Good job, well done!" the neighbors cheer.

Trucks return to the old fire hall,
And from them weary people crawl . . .

...take off their coats, their pants, their hats,
Clean up their trucks...themselves...that's that.

And then they hope to sleep till noon,
As morning puts away the moon.